W9-BLP-731

VALERIE
AND THE
SILVER PEAR

Benjamin Darling

ILLUSTRATED BY *Dan Lane*

FOUR WINDS PRESS ❉ NEW YORK

MAXWELL MACMILLAN CANADA   TORONTO
MAXWELL MACMILLAN INTERNATIONAL
NEW YORK   OXFORD   SINGAPORE   SYDNEY

Special thanks to Ann Hodgman for her pie-making expertise and recipe

Four Winds Press
Macmillan Publishing Company
866 Third Avenue
New York, NY 10022

Maxwell Macmillan Canada, Inc.
1200 Eglinton Avenue East, Suite 200
Don Mills, Ontario M3C 3N1

Macmillan Publishing Company is part of
the Maxwell Communication Group of Companies.
First edition
Printed and bound in the United States of America

10   9   8   7   6   5   4   3   2   1

The text of this book is set in 16 point Cochin.
The illustrations are rendered in watercolor and colored pencil.
Book design by Christy Hale

Library of Congress Cataloging-in-Publication Data
Darling, Benjamin, date.
Valerie and the silver pear / Benjamin Darling ; illustrated by Dan Lane.
p.   cm.
Summary: Valerie and her grandfather preserve the memory of
her grandmother by making pear pies together. Includes a recipe for
pear pie.
ISBN 0-02-726100-X
[1. Grandparents—Fiction.   2. Baking—Fiction.   3. Pear—
Fiction.]   I. Lane, Dan, date. ill.   II. Title.
PZ7.D2477Val   1992
[E]—dc20   90-24945

For Joe and Tommie Ross
Special thanks to Brooke

—D.L.

Summer days Valerie liked to visit her grandfather. He lived on the edge of town in the house he and Valerie's grandmother had bought when they were first married. The house had a big backyard with a pear tree, a cherry tree, and an apple tree.

Grandpa had planted the trees the first year he and
Valerie's grandmother had lived there. Grandma had loved
fruits. She would make pear pies and cherry preserves,
and, of course, eat apples fresh off the tree.

On this particular summer day, Valerie and her grandfather made their lunch of cheese sandwiches and apple juice and took it out to eat on the back porch. They ate and looked out at the fruit trees in the backyard. They didn't say anything for a very long time, until Grandfather told Valerie a story.

"It's a funny thing, Valerie, but most years that pear tree grows a single silver pear. Just under the skin it's solid silver—very beautiful. Your grandmother liked to give them away. Once she even sent one to the queen of England."

"Do you think you and I could look for the silver pear this year, Grandpa?"

"What an excellent idea, Valerie. You'd be just the person to find it."

Grandfather went to the shed and got two bushel baskets. The pear tree was tall and beautiful, heavy with fruit, and they quickly filled the first basket. Valerie picked the lower pears; Grandfather got the higher-up ones. For the second basket, Valerie sat on her grandfather's shoulders. He held the basket, and she dropped the pears down into it. They had to get the ladder out of the shed to pick the very last pears from the top branches of the tree.

They took the two baskets of pears into the kitchen. Then they carefully washed each pear and laid it on the kitchen table. When they were done, Grandpa made some iced tea.

"Next time you come, we'll have plenty of good, sweet pears. They should be nice and ripe by then," he said.

"Can we look for the silver pear then?" Valerie asked.

"Certainly we will," Grandpa replied. "And maybe we can figure out something to do with all the pears that aren't silver."

When Valerie went to her grandfather's house again, he showed her a picture of the queen. The writing on the picture said, "Thank you for the lovely silver pear. I shall always cherish it. The Queen."

"I found this when I was digging around up in the attic. I thought you might like to see it. Your grandmother never wanted to hang it up. She was like that."

"Like what, Grandpa?"

"Shy, she was always shy about the silver pears. When we found the first one I wanted to call the newspapers, tell everyone. But your grandmother quietly wrapped it up and sent it off to a charity."

"Oh, Grandpa, let's hurry and check the ones we picked."

"Okay, but first we need to take a look at your grandmother's recipe book."

Together they looked over the tattered old book and found the pear recipes.

"Pear jam is no fun to make," said Grandpa.

"I don't like canned pears." Valerie made a funny face.

"How about pies?" Grandpa asked. "I always loved your grandmother's pear pies."

They both agreed that pear pies were the most fun to make and the best to eat.

"First we must make a list of things to get at the store," Grandpa said. "How many pies will we make?"

"I counted the pears! We have forty-three, Grandpa, and our recipe says we need five pears for each pie."

"Which will make eight pies, plus one pear for you to eat, one for me to eat, and one extra," Grandpa said. "That must be the silver one."

Carefully, they made out a shopping list: flour, sugar, butter, four lemons, and a few other things. They took the list to the grocery store. Valerie pushed the cart, and Grandpa picked out the ingredients.

"I think this is the kind of butter your grandmother always used." Grandpa wasn't quite sure.

"Yes, she told me once that it was the best kind," Valerie assured him.

When they had finished getting all the other groceries they needed, they went over to the produce section to buy lemons. Valerie looked at the pears for sale.

"These are nice," she said, "but ours are *much* better."

"You can't beat what you grow in your own backyard," Grandpa told her.

On the way home from the store, Grandpa told Valerie another story.

"Valerie, you know, I'd almost forgotten. One year, early on, we couldn't decide who to give the pear to. Finally, your grandmother decided to let fate decide for us. We were going to the seaside that summer. Your grandmother had never seen the ocean, but she had read a lot about it, and she knew about messages in bottles."

"You put the pear in a bottle?" Valerie was surprised.

"Well, not exactly a bottle. We used a big mason jar. Your grandmother put in a note that said, 'This is a silver pear. We hope you will like it.' Something simple like that. We sealed up the jar with wax and took it on down to the ocean with us, and when we were sure the tide was going out, we tossed it in as far as we could."

"Whoever found it must have been surprised," said Valerie.

"They sure must have. We had fun sometimes trying to think who it could have been."

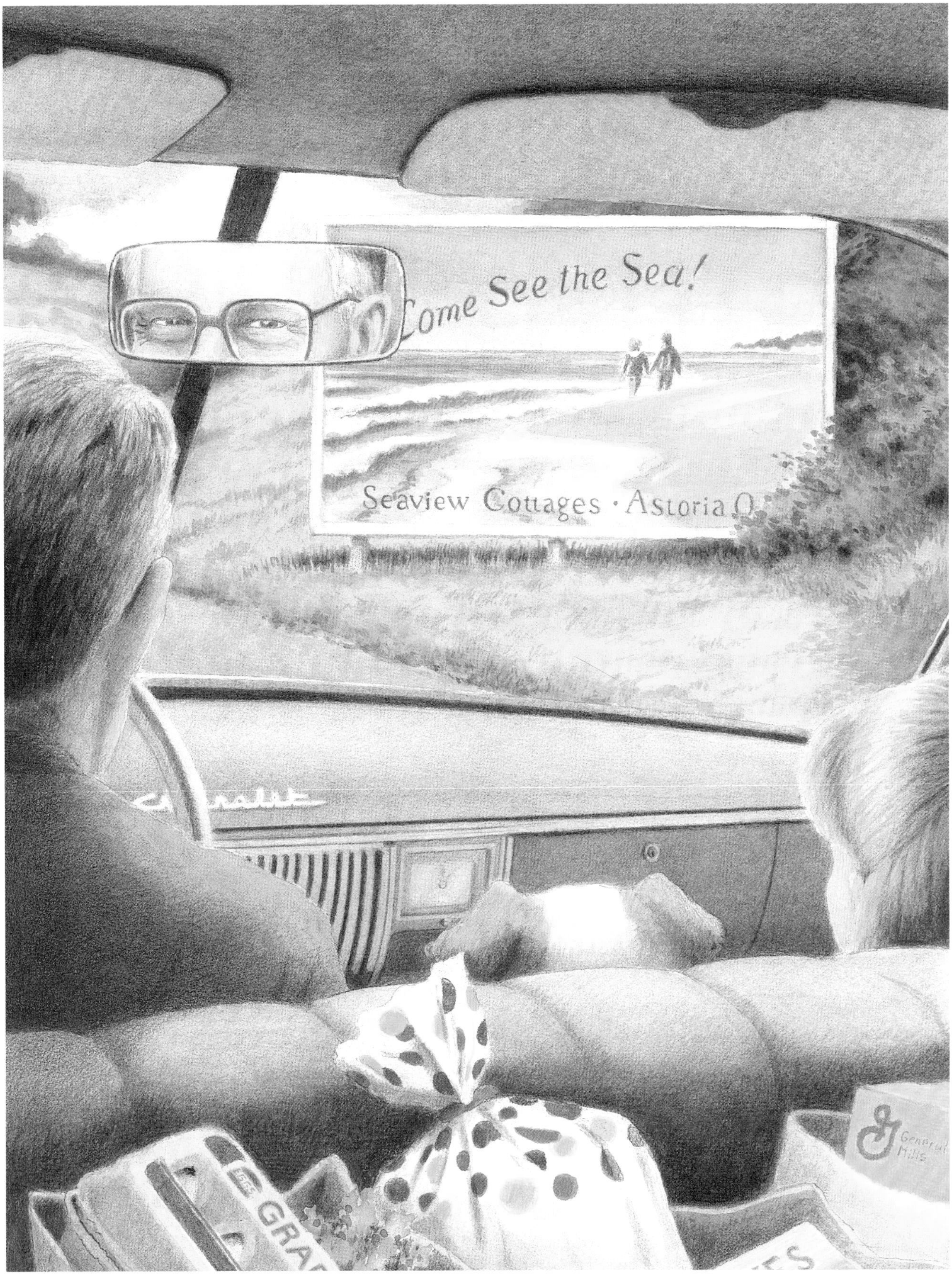
Come See the Sea!
Seaview Cottages · Astoria O
General Mills

When they arrived back at Grandfather's house, Valerie helped to put away all the things they had bought.

"There, now we can bake tomorrow," Valerie said triumphantly.

Grandfather walked Valerie home, where he was invited to stay for dinner. They told the family that they had important things to do the next day, but nobody could guess what. Valerie and Grandpa wanted the pies to be a surprise.

Valerie arrived earlier than usual at her grandfather's house the next day. Grandfather made some lemonade, and they looked over the recipe for pear pie. It looked more complicated now. Where to begin?

"I think we should start by making the crust," said Grandfather.

"Yes, that's the way Grandma did it," Valerie agreed.

They decided to make enough for four pies at a time. That was as many as the oven could hold.

"While the first four are cooking, we can mix up the ingredients for the other four," Valerie decided.

Grandpa measured out the flour, butter, and salt into a big bowl while Valerie read to him from Grandma's recipe book. They mixed in the butter and water, following the recipe exactly. But when they tried to roll out the dough, it wouldn't stick together. It just crumbled.

"What should we do, Grandpa?" Valerie asked.

"Let's call the library. Surely somebody there can help us."
The librarian didn't even have to look in a book to help
Valerie and Grandfather. She just told them to add a little
more water to their dough and to put it in the refrigerator
for thirty minutes.

While the dough chilled, they carefully peeled each pear. They finished peeling each of the forty pears but still hadn't found the silver one.

"It must be one of the last three," said Grandpa.

Fixing the pears was easy. They cut them up and mixed them with sugar, lemon juice, cornstarch, nutmeg, and a spice called mace. Then they took the dough out of the refrigerator and rolled it out. It worked perfectly this time. They made four crusts and divided the pear mixture equally between them, dotting the pears with little bits of butter and placing the top crusts on carefully.

As the first four pies went into the oven, Valerie looked at Grandpa.

"Boy, making pies is hard work."

"Sure is," agreed Grandpa. "And we still have four more to go."

But they got to work again, and the second batch went much faster than the first. They took the first four pies out of the oven to cool, and put in the second four.

"Whew!" said Grandpa. "That was tough. I'm hungry."

"How about those last three pears?" Valerie asked.

"Good idea; it's about time. Buddy!" Grandfather called to his dog.

Grandfather cut a little piece off one of the pears and put it in Buddy's bowl, and he ate it up.

"Too much pear isn't good for a dog, but he does love pears," Grandfather explained.

He handed Valerie one of the two remaining pears. They carefully bit into them, not wanting to hurt their teeth on the silver. Both of them found only fruit underneath the skin. It was delicious fruit, though, and they ate up their pears.

"Why do you think there was no silver pear this year, Grandpa?" Valerie asked.

"I honestly don't know, Valerie. Your grandmother always found one. Although one year it looked as if she wouldn't. There was a late frost, and all the pears froze up when they were just tiny. They never grew any bigger than the tip of my finger. We had pretty much given up on silver pears that year. Until one day I was out mowing the lawn, and one of those tiny pears fell and hit me on the head. I could tell by the way it smarted that it was no ordinary pear, and sure enough, it was the silver one.

"I never told your grandmother, but when her birthday came around I had it put on a little bracelet and gave it to her. I wonder if you would like to have it?"

Grandpa pulled Grandma's bracelet with the tiny silver pear out of his pocket and put it on Valerie's wrist.

"Thank you, Grandpa!"

The oven timer went off, and they hurried to get the last of the pies out of the oven.

As the pies cooled, Valerie said, "You know what I think, Grandpa?"

"No, what?"

"I think it's not a silver pear this year. I think it's switched to a silver apple. I love apples."

"Of course! That must be it. Perhaps we could start on the apples tomorrow."

Valerie and Grandfather each got a big helping of pie and sat down at the kitchen table to eat. After a few big bites, Grandpa said, "Your grandmother would have been proud of this pie."

"It's delicious!" Valerie agreed.

"Valerie, did I ever tell you about the time her apple butter won the blue ribbon at the state fair?"

"No, but I'd love to hear about it, Grandpa. Is apple butter hard to make?" Valerie asked.

"We'll have to find the recipe and see. But first, let's have another piece of this fine pie."

Note: This is the recipe Grandpa and Valerie used. With the help of an adult, you can make your own pear pies!

PEAR PIE

Ingredients

Makes one 9″ pie

Piecrust for 2-crust 9″ pie
1 tablespoon melted butter

Filling

5 large pears
Juice of half a lemon
A pinch of salt
A pinch of nutmeg
½ teaspoon mace
½ cup sugar
1 tablespoon cornstarch (1½ tablespoons
    if the pears are very juicy)
2 tablespoons butter, cut into bits

Directions

Preheat the oven to 375°F.

Divide the pie dough into 2 circles, one slightly larger than the other, and chill for 30 minutes. On a lightly floured surface, roll out the larger of the 2 pastry balls into a circle that is 2″ wider than the pie pan and ⅛″-¼″ thick. Fit it gently into a greased 9″ pie pan and trim the edges to leave a ½″ overhang. Brush all over with the melted butter, which will help to keep the crust flaky. Chill while you prepare the filling.

Peel, core, and slice the pears. Toss them gently with the lemon juice, salt, nutmeg, and mace. Stir the sugar and cornstarch together, add to the pears, and toss thoroughly once more. Let the mixture sit while you prepare the top crust.

Roll the smaller ball of pastry into a circle that is 1″ larger than the pan and ⅛″ thick. Spoon the pear mixture into the chilled bottom crust and dot with the butter. With a finger dipped in water, moisten the edge of the bottom crust slightly. Place the top crust over the pie and tuck its edges under the bottom crust, pressing the 2 crusts firmly to make them adhere. Press the tines of a fork around the edge of the pie for decoration. Trim off any extra bits of dough, leaving a ¼″ overhang. (The crust will shrink slightly during baking.) Cut 8 vents in the top crust to let out the steam while the pie is baking.

Place the pie on a cookie sheet and put it on a rack in the lower third of the oven. Bake the pie for 50 minutes, or until well browned. (If the edges of the pie are browning too fast, cover them with foil.) Cool slightly before serving.